BEAUTY AND THE BEAST

A Fairy Extravaganza

IN TWO ACTS

BY J.R. PLANCHE

Published by Left of Brain Books

ISBN 978-1-396-32106-1

First Edition

Table of Contents

CAST OF CHARACTERS.

	Covent Garden, 1841.	*Olympic, 1842.*
Beauty .	.Madame Vestris.	Mrs. Timm.
The Beast, .	.Mr. W. Harrison.	Mr. Walcot.
alias Prince Azor		
Sir Aldgate Pump,	." J. Bland.	" Nickinson.
(Beauty's Father)		
John Quill .	." Harley.	" Mitchell.
Dressalinda .	.Miss Rainforth.	Miss Mary Taylor.
Marrygolda .	." Grant.	Mrs. Mossop.
Queen of Roses	." Lee.	Miss Clarke.
Zephyrs .	.Mr. Marshall, &c.	" Roberts, &c.

COSTUMES.

SIR ALDGATE PUMP. — Red tab jacket and trunks, large puffs, red stockings, long toed shoes, very small sugar loaf hat, and single feather, outré wig.

JOHN QUILL. — Same style of dress as Sir Aldgate, but plainer.

THE BEAST. — Flesh arms and legs, bear skin body, hands and feet, large head and mask.

BEAUTY. — Stuff petticoat, tuck-up gown, high neck frill, sugar loaf hat, black stockings, high heeled shoes.

MARRYGOLDA. — Ditto.

DRESSALINDA. — Ditto.

QUEEN OF ROSES. — Short white dress, trimmed with roses, wreath of roses on head.

NOBLES. — Rich shape dresses.

EXITS AND ENTRANCES.

R. means *Right*;   L. *Left*;   R.D. *Right Door;*   L.D. *Left Door*;   S.E. *Second Entrance*;
U.E. *Upper Entrance*;   M.D. *Middle Door.*

RELATIVE POSITIONS.

R., means *Right*;   L., *Left*;   C., *Centre*;   R.C., *Right of Centre*;   L.C., *Left of Centre.*

N.B. Passages marked with Inverted Commas, *are usually omitted in the representation.*

BEAUTY AND THE BEAST.

ACT I.

Scene I. — *A Bower of Roses, not by Bendemeer's Stream.*

Enter a Troop of Zephyrs, to the "Gavotte de Vestris."

Zephyr. How's this! what, still asleep, my Rosy Posies?
      Come ope your eyes and blow your little noses.
      Not a leaf stirring yet — why, gracious powers,
      Are you aware the time of day, my flowers?
      Have you forgotten that your Queen proposes
      This day to ope the Parliament of Roses?

CHORUS OF ROSES. — *Ditto of Bridesmaids. — "Der Frieschutz."*

      Sweet Zephyr, don't make such a breeze,
      We're rather late this morning,
      But don't be angry, if you please,
      We shan't take long adorning;
      Sleep, you know, will sometimes thus enthrall us,
      You should earlier call us.

[*Music. — The Queen of Roses appears.*]

Zephyr. Behold your Sovereign! Silence, all and each,
      To hear Her Majesty's most flow'ry speech.

Queen. My Buds and Blossoms, I rejoice to say,
      That I continue to receive each day
      Assurances from all the foreign flowers
      Of their good will towards these happy bowers—

I have concluded, on the best foundations,
A treaty with the king of the Carnations,
And trust ere long to lay the leaves before you.
I'm sorry now to be obliged to bore you
On an old subject, but, for your digestion
At Easter, we must have an Easter Question—
And, on my faithful Roses I depend
To bring the matter to a happy end.
The facts are these: a youth of royal race,
Of noble mind and matchless form and face,
Has been transformed by a malicious fairy,
Into an ugly monster, huge and hairy;
And must remain a downright beast outside,
'Till some fair maid consents to be his bride.
My Buds and Blossoms, you will take that measure,
Of course, which best may work your Sovereign's pleasure—
Which is, that through a Rose's meditation,
The Prince may be restored to form and station.
Ere nightfall, I expect you'll break the spell,
And so, my Buds and Blossoms, fare ye well.

CHORUS. — ("Coal Black Rose.")

Queen of Roses, we'll take care
To lay before this honorable House the affair;
If we can get two acts passed, without its being nettled,
The Beast will be *re-formed*, and the Easter question settled;
No rose, here that blows,
Will vote against a measure, ma'am that you propose.
[*The Scene closes.*]

Scene II. — *Interior of "Pump's Folly."*

Enter Marrygolda *and* Dressalinda, *R.*

Marry.   Oh, sister! sister! times have altered sadly,

To think we should live poorly—

Dressal.   And dress badly!

Marry.   We who have banqueted in fair Guildhall.

Dressal.   We who have opened Easter Monday's ball—

Marry.   The daughters of Sir Aldgate Pump, Lord Mayor of London
once—

Dressal.   And now, though past the chair,
A Knight and Alderman, who might again
Wear o'er the velvet gown the golden chain,
Had not malicious Fortune, at one blow,
Ruined the famous firm of Pump & Co.

Marry.   Out on the jade! could she none else have fixed on
To banish from Threadneedle Street to Brixton—
Sad change from merriment to melancholy,
From lordly Mansion House to poor "Pump's Folly."

Dressal.   It makes me mad to hear our sister Beauty
Say we should be content, and prate of duty,
And resignation, and that sort of stuff —
She thinks a grogram gown is fine enough.

Marry.   And so, it is for her—to scrub the floor in,
To cook the dinner, or to ope the door in.
That's all she's fit for — with her wax-doll's face,
What matters what she thinks in any case!
We are her elders, and her betters, too,
And need more ornament—than she can do.

Dressal.   Here comes papa—and in a mighty hurry!

Enter Sir Aldgate Pump, *hastily, L., in great agitation, with an open letter in his head.*

Sir Ald.   Oh, Gog and Magog!

Marry.   Bless me, what a flurry
You seem in, sir—is anything amiss?
Or have you heard good news?

Sir Ald.   Girls, come and kiss
Your happy father. Pumps are up! Behold
This precious letter! List, whilst I unfold
The glorious tidings—Fortune, in her sport,
Has brought the good ship "Polly" into Port!

Dressal.   The barque you thought was lost on some vile rock?

Sir Ald.   Is safe in Plymouth Sound.

Marry.   You're sure, sir?

Sir Ald.   Cock!

Dressal.   Why, she was thought the richest of your fleet.

Sir Ald.   Her cargo's worth would buy all Lombard Street!

Marry.   Then we again in gilded coach shall ride.

Dressal.   And wear the finest clothes in all Cheapside.

Sir Ald.   Again, a roaring trade on 'Change I'll drive!
But I must hence with speed, so look alive—
Where is my youngest hope, my beauty fair?

Marry.   I'm sure, pa, I don't know.

Dressal.   And I don't care.
[Retires up.]

Enter Beauty, singing, R.

AIR. — BEAUTY. — *("Gondolier, row.")*
Gondolier, row, row,
Gondolier, row, row;
'Tis a pretty air,
I do declare,
But it haunts a body so,
Gondolier, row, row,
Gondolier, row, row;
At work or play,
By night or day,
I sing it wher'er I go.

Beauty.   Good morning, sir.

Sir Ald.   Rejoice, my child, for now,
The "Polly's" safe in port.

Beauty.   You don't say so.

Sir Ald.   Read! —you can read?

Beauty.   Both print and written hand.

Sir Ald.   Accomplished creature! —and can understand
What you do read?

Beauty.   Affirm that quite, I wouldn't—

7

Because, at times, e'en those who write it couldn't!

Sir Ald.   Where's my ex-clerk and faithful drudge, John Quill?

Enter John Quill, *L.*

John Q.   Here, master. I am your remainder still.

Sir Ald.   Run to the "Goat in Boots."

John Q.   Yes, master—Dot
And carry one—
[Going.]

Sir Ald.   Stop! you've not heard for what.
Order a chaise and four—and mind, John, you
Must travel with me—

John Q.   Dot and carry two.
[Exit, L.]

Sir Ald.   Rot your arithmetic, and stir your stumps—
This is a glorious day, girl, for the Pumps!

Beauty.   Where go you, father?

Sir Ald.   To the ship, my dear,
To land her cargo and the customs clear.

Dressal.   You'll bring some present home, I hope, for me.

Sir Ald.   With all my heart, my love—what shall it be?

Dressal.   Oh, any trifle that falls in your way—
A hundred guinea shawl, suppose we say.

Sir Ald.	A hundred—Humph—but then, your sisters, too.
Marry.	Oh, sir, I wouldn't think of asking you To buy a shawl for me—that were too rash— I'll take a hundred guineas, sir, in cash.
Sir Ald.	Considerate child! But first, love, I must net 'em. In the meanwhile, I'll wish that you may get 'em. But what says Beauty? is my pet so happy, That she's no boon to ask of her own Pappy? You've heard the choice of your two sisters here, One's for mere cash, the other for Cashmere. What says my duck?
Beauty.	[*Aside.*] If nothing, I suppose They'll call me proud. [*Aloud.*] Well, bring me, sir, a rose.
Sir Ald.	A rose!
Beauty.	Yes—in our little garden here, There is not one at this time of the year; And I'm so fond of roses.
Dressal.	}
	} Well, if ever!
Marry.	}
Sir Ald.	Only a flower! — Nonsense, child — endeavour To think of something else.
Beauty.	No, sir — 'twill be Enough to prove that you have thought of me When far away.
Dressal.	}
	} Sweet sentimental soul!

Marry.   }

Sir Ald.   I'll bring one, though I scratch from pole to pole to find it.

Re-enter John Quill, *L., with a neck shawl.*

John Q.   Sir, they've brought over the shay.

Sir Ald.   Brought over! brought it to the door, you'd say —

John Q.   Yes, sir.

Sir Ald.   Are all my things well packed behind?

John Q.   I've added up, sir, all that I can find,
And here is the grand total.
[*Shows shawl.*]
Sir Ald.   A small stock — it
Won't take much room up — put it in your pocket.
And now, farewell, my darlings! Behave pretty,
I'll come back and astonish all the City.

QUINTETTE. — ("*The Fox jumped over.*")

John Q.   I've just looked over the garden gate,
And sorry am to observe it snows;

Sir Ald.   Oho! does it so, John? I'll wrap up my pate
One last embrace and away we *go.*

Beauty.   Wrap, Father, wrap this round your chest,
[*Taking shawl from John Quill.*]
The days caught cold, I do protest,
For, ah! you hear, it blows, it snows;

10

Sir Ald.	One last embrace and away we *go.*
Dressal.	Beaux will swarm —
John Q.	Multiplication —
Marry.	Cash be plenty —
John Q.	Sweet addition —
All.	Now without more conversation, Here at once we part.
John Q.	Division.

[*Exeunt,* Sir Aldgate *and* John Quill , *L.,* Dressalinda *and* Marrygolda, *R.]*

Beauty. More snow! He'll have sharp weather, there's no doubt;
 But Pa was always fond of "cold without."

AIR. — BEAUTY. — (*"Happy Land."*)
Father bland, Father bland,
Blander none could ever be,
Come again, come again,
And bring a rose to me.
You I love, and you I prize,
You're the joy of Beauty;
Your merry heart, and laughing eyes,
Still make affection duty.
Father bland, Father bland,
While the sun shines make your hay,
But let me hear, soon again,
The sound of thy post-shay.

Lirala,
The sound of thy return post-shay.
Forced to go through frost and snow,
Far from thine own dwelling,
Whether thou'lt come back or no,
Really there's no telling.
Father bland, & c.
[*Exit Beauty, R.*]

SCENE III. — *A Forest. — Snow Storm. — A crash without,* R.S.E.

Sir Ald.   [*Without.*] Holloh! — confusion! — help! — holloh, John Quill!

John Q.   Here, master!

Enter Sir Aldgate *and* John Quill, R.S.E.

Mercy on us, what a spill.

Sir Ald.   The leaders shied away at that confounded drover.

John Q.   Fours in a ditch go once, sir, and two over.

Sir Ald.   "Go once," indeed — a very pretty go —
And fancy, too, a heavy fall in the snow!
As the Scotch gentleman says in the play,
"What wood is this before us?"

John Q.   I can't say.

Sir Ald.   It isn't Birnam — that's as clear as light.

John Q.   Why, no; it's more like Freez'em to my sight.

12

Sir Ald.   John — we are in a pretty situation.

John Q.   I'm out completely in my calculation.

Sir Ald.   Fate seems determined, John, to use me queerly,
The chaise is broken all to shivers nearly.

John Q.   I shouldn't mind the shivering of the shay,
If we could keep from shivering here all day.

Sir Ald.   Is there no friendly power to shield or spare
A Knight and Alderman, who's been Lord Mayor?
Protecting Genius, to my rescue fly.

John Q.   Law! — you've no more a Genius, sir, then I.
[*The Scene changes slowly to a beautiful Garden, with a view of a Castle in the background.*]

Sir Ald.   The deuce I haven't! See, my prayer is heard
By some kind spirit, never mind the word;
The sky is clearing, it has left off snowing;
The wood is "all a-growing, all a-blowing;"
And yonder, I behold a castle fair,
Such as I've built too often in the air.

John Q.   Oh, Bonnycastle! Sir, I ask your pardon,
Your genius has cast up a lovely garden,
With beds of roses, and with bowers of myrtle,
Where the fond turtle —

Sir Ald.   Oh, don't mention turtle!
I'm famished, and would give, I know not what,
For a good quart from Birch's, smoking hot.
        [*A table rises with a bason of soup on it,* c.]
Amazement! at my wish, a bason see!

John Q.   Oh, Master, wish again, a pint for me!
        [*A small bason appears on the table, c.*]

Sir Ald.   'Tis there!

John Q.   Now was't because I wished, or you?
        Perhaps I've got a little genius, too;
        I'll try — a nice French roll, sir, if you please;
           [*A basket with bread rises on table, c.*]
        Now, that I call getting one's bread with ease,
        And that's what geniuses don't often do.

Sir Ald.   This is the *best bred* one I ever knew.
        Delicious soup!

John Q.   I say, good master mine,
        Suppose we both wish for a little wine.

Sir Ald.   With all my heart.

John Q.   What shall it be, Champagne?

Sir Ald.   Stop! Punch with turtle — Punch *a la* Romaine.
          [*The punch rises — they drink.*]
        Perfect!

John Q.   I should say quite. Some more to eat?

Sir Ald.   A slice of venison, now, would be a treat.
  [*The soup is replaced by a silver dish with a lamp under it, and filled with
               hashed venison.*]
        A better hash ne'er smoked upon a table.

John Q.   If this were told, they'd count it a mere fable.

Sir Ald.   Now, if you'd fancy some superior sherry?

John Q.   Bless you, I do!
          [*A decanter of sherry replaces the punch. — Sir Ald. drinks.*]
          Is it superior?

Sir Ald.   [*Setting down his glass.*] Very. [*Rises.*]

          John, I feel all the better for my lunch.

John Q.   My head is none the better for that punch.

Sir Ald.   Come, let us try if we can find our way.

John Q.   D'ye think, sir, that there's anything to pay?

Sir Ald.   I don't know, but I won't wish for the bill.

John Q.   No, don't; the gentleman might take it ill.
          Which is the way out, I can't tell, can you?
          My eyes are multiplying all by two.

Sir Ald.   I say, John, Beauty asked me for a rose;
          I'll take her one of these.

John Q.   Yes, do.

Sir Ald.   Here goes!

DUET. — Sir Aldgate and John Quill. — (*"I know a Bank."*)
          I see a bank, whereon a fine one blows,
          It can't be wrong to pluck it, I suppose,
          When 'tis by Beauty seen, if we get home tonight,

So, fond of flowers, she'll dance, sir, with delight.
   [Sir Aldgate gathers a rose. — Thunder, lightning, &c.]

Enter the Beast, R.S.E., with an enormous club.

   AIR. — Beast and Chorus. [Chorus behind the Scenes.] —
                (*"Garde a vous."*)

Tremble you, tremble you,
Who dare to pluck my roses?
I'll tear ye limb from limb, and with your bones the
churchyard strew.
Tremble you, tremble you!
On turtle soup and punch, rogues,
You've made a hearty lunch, rogues,
Now I will lunch on you, lunch on you, lunch on you.

Chorus.   On turtle soup, &c.

Beast.   Is this your gratitude for lunching gratis?
Trespass on my preserves! Ohe jam satis!
       [Puts his club on Pump's toes.]
But I will have your bones ground into dust.
And make a pie of you, with your own crust.

Sir Ald.   Mercy, great King of Clubs! one moment pause.

Beast.   Well, take a rule, then, rascals, to show cause
Why I should not beat, with this oaken plant,
The brains of both out —

John Q.   Brains from one you can't.

Sir Ald.   Pity the sorrows of a poor old Pump,
Whose trembling knees against each other thump
And listen, with a kind attentive ear,

Whilst he explains what now seems rather queer.

> AIR. — Sir Aldgate. — (*"Under the Rose."*)
> Great sir, don't fly out, for a trifle, this,
> What harm have I done, sir? one rose you can't miss.
> Don't make, if you please, sir, so fierce a grimace,
> You'd have done the same thing, had you been in my place.
> I'm a family man, sir, fair daughters I've three.
> There's one they call Beauty, because she's like me;
> Her pleading resistless, what heart could oppose;
> "Papa," said the pretty girl, "bring me a rose."

Beast.   I don't believe a word of this affair.

Sir Ald.   As I'm an Alderman, and have been Mayor,
You may depend on the account I give.

John Q.   As I'm a Liveryman who hopes to live,
If you'll examine his account, you'll find it
Correct.

Beast.   Your promise, then, and oath to bind it,
That you will bring that daughter here to die
Instead of you —

Sir Ald.   To die! Oh, my!

John Q.   Oh, cry!

Beast.   Come, make your mind up quickly, you or her.
Decide! It's immaterial quite to me.

Sir Ald.   My lord!

Beast.   I'm not a lord, sir, I'm a beast.

Sir Ald.   You wouldn't have us call you one, at least?

Beast.   I would; I like the truth; I'm a plain creature.

John Q.   The plainest that I ever saw in feature.

Beast.   Is it a bargain? Speak, I wait to strike it.

Sir Ald.   I'll go and ask my daughter if she'd like it.

Beast.   Of course, man, that's exactly what I meant;
I wouldn't eat her without her consent.

Sir Ald.   If *I* object, then, sir, you won't eat me?

Beast.   Oh! that's another matter quite, you see;
Come, swear you will return in either case.

Sir Ald.   I do.

Beast.   By what?

Sir Ald.   The City Sword and Mace!

Beast.   'Tis well, away! I shall expect you back
In half-an-hour—

Sir Ald.   In half-an-hour? Good luck!
How far are we from home?

Beast.   Four leagues and more,
But here's an omnibus goes past your door,
And only stops to take up and set down.

[A Car, on which is written, "Time Flies. No Stoppages," with a Zephyr for driver, and another for cad, enters, L.U.E.]

Cad.   Now, sir, Bank! City! Bank! Going up to Town?

Sir Ald.   *[Getting in, followed by John Q.]* Pump's Folly, Brixton.

Beast.   *[To Cad.]* With the speed of light.
[To Sir A.]   In half-an-hour?

Sir Ald.   Certainly!

Cad.   All right! *[They fly off, R.—Exit Beast, L.U.E.]*

SCENE IV. — Interior of Cottage, as before.

Enter Marrygolda, R.

AIR. – Marrygolda. — (*"'Tis really very strange."*)
 'Tis really very strange,
 But people say, on 'Change,
 That some ill-natured folks
 Have dared Papa to hoax,
 And that in Plymouth Sound
 No Polly's to be found.
 'Tis really very strange,
 But that's the news on 'Change.
 They also say, on 'Change,
 What's even still more strange,
 That Beauty's above par,
 And we at discount are;
 Now, if this should be true,
 Oh, dear! what shall we do;
 'Tis really very strange,
 But that's the news on 'Change.

19

[The Gate Bell rings, L.]

Enter Dressalinda, R.

Dressal. Hark! there's the gate bell! why, who can it be?

Marry. Beauty!

Enter Beauty, R.

How now? why don't you run and see?

Beauty. I'm going, sister.
    [*Exit, L.*]

Dressal. Going! — stir, then, stir!
She really wants a maid to wait on her.

Marry. What has she done today?

Dressal. Her work — no more.

Marry. The lazy hussy!

Re-enter Beauty, L.

Dressal. Well, who's at the door?

Beauty. My father! — in his habit, as he started.

Marry. Can it be possible?

Dressal. The dear departed!

Enter Sir Aldgate and John Quill, L. — Beauty gets a chair for Sir Aldgate.

Marry. Returned so soon!

John Q.	Returned like a bad penny.
Dressal.	You've got my shawl?
Sir Ald.	No — for I've not seen any.
Marry.	The money, sir, for me, at least, you brought —
Sir Ald.	I've seen no money —
John Q.	Dot and carry naught.
Dressal.	No shawl!
Marry.	No money! what a horrid bore.
Sir Ald.	I've brought a rose for Beauty — nothing more.
Beauty.	Oh, thanks! I hope it has not cost you dear —
Sir Ald.	Only my life, my love!
Beauty.	What's this I hear?

Sir Ald.   "Forlorn, deserted, melancholy, slow,"
(For we'd been overturned, love, in the snow,)
We wandered – like two large Babes in the Wood,
Except, that no Cock Robins brought us food —
When, lo! a splendid mansion rose to sight,
Which, talk of Robins, George alone could write
A true description of — Meand'ring streams,
Perennial bowers that mocked the poets' dream
Surpassing all that e'er that great magician
Submitted yet to public competition!
Nor was the eye alone allowed to feed,

Turtle and Punch were furnished us with speed.
Nothing to pay — Turtle without a bill,
And Punch that made a Judy of John Quill!
John, tell the rest — for out I cannot bring it.

John Q.   I haven't heart to say it, sir.

Beauty.   Then sing it.

John Q.   I'll try — perhaps the air may do you good.

Beauty.   I shouldn't wonder really if it would.

AIR. — John Quill . — (*"I have plucked the fairest flower."*)

He thought of Beauty's flower,
And he popped into a bower,
And he plucked the fairest rose
That he found beneath his nose;
But scarce had he done so,
When a monster, black as crow,
Like an arrow from a bow,
Flew out and cried, Holloa
Here's a very pretty go, a very pretty go,
You rascals, oh!
You have spoiled my flower-show,
And to pot you both shall go
In a squad-pie, oh!"
Then we fell upon our knees,
And we said, "Sir. if you please,
We did *not* mean to offend,
'Twas to please a lady friend:"
On which he answered, "Oh!
If, indeed, the truth be so,
You'll be good enough to go,

And just let that lady know,
She must pay for Pump & Co.
Pay for Pump & Co."
'Twas a horrid blow,
And it made us very low,
And we've come to let you know,
With a sad heigho!

Beauty.   The horrid brute!

Marry.   How could you be so silly?

Dressal.   What was he like?

John Q.   The Brown Bear, Piccadilly.

Sir A.   To cut my story short — or you, or I, —

Beauty.   Must for that brute be made into squab pie.

Beauty.   Oh, horror! – make a squab pie of my father!
             I'd rather — oh, I don't know what I'd rather.

Marry.   I hope, Miss Beauty, you are satisfied.

Dressal.   Your rose has proved a nice thorn in your side.

Marry.   Our father's death will lie, miss, at your door.

Beauty.   Never! I'll die a hundred deaths before.

Sir Ald.   My noble child! [*Embraces her.*]

John Q.   The very Queen of Trumps!

Sir Ald.   Oh, fate! come to the succour of the Pumps!
              Let not the flower of our ancient race
              Be made into a pie before my face.

John Q.   "Time flies!" — you told the omnibus to call
              As it went back.

Dressal.   This time do get my shawl —

Marry.   And if you can but bring me fifty pounds,
              Or only five-and-twenty, sir.

Sir Ald.   Odd zounds!
              Is this a time about such trash to tease —
              When your poor sister —

Enter Cad, *L.*

Cad.   Now, sir, if you please. [*Exit, L.*]

Beauty.   Farewell, dear sisters, I forgive you both —
              Go, father.

Sir Ald.   And fare worse — oh, cruel oath.

John Q.   Don't cast up hope, dear master, fate may save her,
              And strike a balance yet, sir, in our favour.

QUINTETTE. — (*"Mild as the Moonbeams."*)
    To death, per Omnibus, poor Beauty goes,
    And all because her Pa just plucked a rose.
    Mild as the moon, when a cream-cheese she resembles,
    And sweet as sugar plums, Birch's best.

[*Exeunt, Sir Aldgate, John Quill, and Beauty, L., Marrygolda and Dressalinda, R.*]

SCENE V. — *Saloon in the Palace of the Beast.*

Enter the Beast, R.

Beast.   Gallop apace, ye fiery-footed steeds.
Oh, if this little scheme of mine succeeds,
The smile of Beauty will the spell destroy,
And I shall jump out of my skin with joy!

AIR. — BEAST. — *"My love is like a red, red rose."*
I sent my love a red, red rose,
And hoped she would come soon.
She can't be long now, I suppose,
For, by my watch, 'tis noon.
Oh! haste and try, my bonny lass,
In love with me to fall,
And you may find 'twill come to pass,
I'm not a beast at all. My dear, &c.
I know I look a fright, my dear,
But my hopes are high,
There's many a girl has loved, my dear,
A greater brute than me.
Say but you'll wed me, sweet Miss Pump,
And to my own fair Isle,
Out of my skin, for joy, I'll jump,
At least ten thousand miles. My dear, &c.

She comes! – be still, my heart – yes, she is there!
And something like a Beauty, I declare.
Let me retire, nor shock, at first, her sight:
But minister, unseen, to her delight. [*Retires.*]

25

Enter Sir Aldgate, Beauty, and John Quill, L.

Sir Ald.	Well, here we are.
Beauty.	It is a lovely place To live in.
John Q.	Yes, but that's another case — You've come to die.
Beauty.	That makes it rather duller.
Sir Ald.	A horse, my dear, of quite another colour.
John Q.	There's dinner ready, take a mouthful, will you?
Sir Ald.	They'd fatten you, it seems, before they kill you.
Beauty.	The thought quite takes my appetite away.
John Q.	Master, you'll pick a morsel? do, sir, pray.
Sir Ald.	I couldn't touch a bit, 'twonld make me will; There isn't any turtle, is there, Quill?
John Q.	Plenty, both calipash and calipee.
Sir Q.	Indeed! Well, if I must, I must.
Beauty.	Ah, me! I'm getting nervous. [*Noise within, R.*] Ugh, what's that?
John Q.	The Beast — The — the — that is — the founder of the feast.

Enter the Beast, R.

Beast.   Madam, you're welcome; won't you take a seat?

Beauty.   I come, sir, to be eaten, not to eat.

Beast.   And came you, madam, of your own accord? Answer me truly.

Beauty.   Yes, indeed, my lord.

Beast.   Don't call me lord, I bet; I told your father
My title is "The Beast."

Beauty.   Well, if you'd rather —

Beast.   But now to business — I'm overjoyed to know
You came here willingly. Pump, you may go.

CONCERTED PIECE. — Beast and Sir Aldgate. — (*"Begone, dull care."*)

Begone, old Pump,
I prithee, begone from me;
Begone, old Pump,
Thy face let me no more see;
Thy daughter who is tarrying here,
Instead of thee I'll kill;
So begone, old Pump,
And take with thee young John Quill.

When Lord Mayor,
Had any one dared to say
Half that, there
Would have been the deuce to pay.
But, alas, they snap their fingers now,

At Sir Aldgate Pump, and say,
Ex-Lord Mayor,
Like a dog, you have had your day.
[*Exeunt Sir Aldgate and John Quill, L.*]

Beast. Now, madam, we're alone, dismiss your fear,
I trust to make you very happy here;
Although I feel that I could eat you up,
I'd rather *with* you breakfast, dine, and sup,
If you'll permit me, but I won't intrude.
You'll find, hope, my outside only rude;
I beg you'll make yourself at home completely —

Beauty. I never thought a beast could speak so sweetly!

Beast. You find me very hideous, I'm afraid.

Beauty. Why — I —

Beast. Oh, speak out, call a spade a spade;
I like to hear the truth, whate'er it be.

Beauty. Indeed! Oh, there, then, we shall both agree!

Beauty. Did you ever see aught like me?

Beauty. Yes, the What-d'ye'call
They once had at the Surrey Zoological.
Beast. The What-d'ye-call! and *was* that like me?

Beauty. Very.
The great Baboon — they called him "Happy Jerry!"

Beast. Were I *your* "Jerry," I *should* "happy" be!
Oh! could I fancy you could fancy me.

Beauty.	*My* Jerry! nay, in that light, truth to speak,
	There's more of "Bruin" in your looks than "Sneak."

Beast.	This condor's quite enchanting! Matchless fair,
	"Your eyes are loadstars, and your tongue's sweet air,
	More tuneable than lark to shepherd's ear;"
	Allow me to take wine with you —

Beauty.	Oh, dear!

AIR. — BEAST.

Drink to me only with your eyes,
If you object to wine;
But if you'll taste this claret cup,
I think you'll own 'tis fine.
But drink to me only with your eyes,
If you object to wine.

Beast.	'Tis late, and you need rest, I will retire;
	Pray call for anything you may desire;
	Behold your room.

[*Over the door of a room appear, in letters of gold, the words, "Beauty's Apartment."*]

You'll find a wardrobe there,
With every sort of dress, you'd like to wear.
Costumes from every land, North, South, West, East.

Beauty.	Delightful!

Beast.	Good night, Beauty!

Beauty.	Good night, Beast! [*Exit Beast, R.*]
	Well, I declare! a very civil brute!
	If manners make the man, beyond dispute

He must be one; though he doesn't look the part,
He seems a perfect gentleman at heart,
And one that, cruelly, no girl would ere cut,
If he'd just shave his beard, and have his hair cut.
Come, downy sleep, a balm from thee I'll borrow,
And look at all these fine affairs tomorrow.
[*Flings herself on the couch, and falls asleep; the Hall is immediately filled
with Spirits of the Rose and Zephyrs, the Queen of the Roses in the midst.*]

Queen.   Beauty, you've been a good girl, and I'll see
That you're rewarded as you ought to be;
Dance round her couch, ye flowers and spirits bright,
And give her pleasant dreams and slumbers tonight.
[*Tableau.*]

END OF ACT I.

———————

ACT II.

SCENE I. — Beauty's Boudoir, in the Palace of the Beast.
Enter Beauty, *richly attired, L.*

AIR. — BEAUTY. — *"Jim along Josey."*
Oh! Rose, as in yon garden you happened to grow,
Perhaps, my pretty Rosy, its master you know?
He looks like a brute, but he acts like a king,
And – bless me, I scarcely know what 'tis I sing.
Oh, get along, get along, Rosey,
Oh, get along, get along, do.
Poor old Papa he kindly let go,
And he hasn't eaten me — as far as I know;
And if he should really offer, instead,
To marry me — Pshaw what put that in my head.
Go, get along, get along, Rosy,
Go, get along, get along, do.

Enter Beast, *L.*

Beast.   Good morning, fairest Beauty, how d'ye do?

Beauty.   I'm pretty well, I thank you, how are you?

Beast.   Dying for love; I couldn't sleep all night
              For thinking of you.

Beauty.   Oh! you're too polite.
              I've had a nice nap, and such pleasant dreams;
              I've got a fairy friend at court, it seems;
              With loves and graces, all in flowers and wings,

She came last night and said such pretty things.

Beast.   You feel quite happy, then?

Beauty.   Oh, no, not quite!

Beast.   Say, what can make you so?

Beauty.   Dear Beast, a sight
                Of my poor father; I'm afraid he's ill.
                Will you oblige me?

Beast.   Certainly, I will;
                Look in that glass, my charming fair — "Veluti
                In Speculum!" — Behold him there, my Beauty.
[*Crosses, R., and waves his hand. — Music – The Glass expands and shows
the inside of the Cottage, with Sir Aldgate, John Quill, Dressalinda and
                Marrygolda, in a tableau vivant.*]

Beauty.   Oh, dear! he's looking very sad and poorly;
                Could you just let me hear his voice, sir?

Beast.   Surely. [*Waves his hand. Music.*]

                    Sir Aldgate Pump. — [*Sings without.*]
            Oh! where, and oh! where, is my daring Beauty gone?
        She's gone to fight the French for King George upon his throne!
            And it's oh! in my heart, I wish she was safe at home.
                [*Beast waves his hand, and Tableau closes.*]

Beauty.   His mind seems wand'ring!

Beast.   What he calls his mind.

Beauty.   Well, if not very wise, he's very kind,

And loves me dearly; let me go, I pray,
And comfort him —

Beast.   How?

Beauty.   Just to spend the day;
I will return ere Sol sinks in the deep.

Beast.   I dare say — catch a weasel fast asleep —

Beauty.   You doubt my word! — I thought you more gallant.

Beast.   Ask for aught else — but that I cannot grant!

Beauty.   Then you don't love me as you say you do.

Beast.   Not love you! — Oh, my wig and whiskers, who
Ere loved so well as I —

Beauty.   There's no believing
You brutes of men — you're always so deceiving.

Beast.   [*Aside.*] I *am* a beast indeed, to make her cry;
Who pipes so sweet, should never pipe her eye.

Beauty.   My pa will die, and you will be the cause,
My fate is in your hands.

Beast.   [*Holding up his hands.*] Ah!
            [*Looks at her and remains silent.*]

Beauty.   Awful pause!

Beast.   You won't come back again —I know you won't.

Beauty.   I wish I may be shot, then, if I don't.

Beast.   You'll be the death of me, mind, if you stay
             One moment after sunset —

Beauty.   Trust me, pray!

Beast.   Upon your mercy, then, myself I fling,
             And so — to prove my love — behold this ring!
             Don't start — it's not a wedding one —

Beauty.   I vow,
             You made me feel — I — really don't know how.

Beast.   The moment that this ring your finger's fixed on,
             Hey, presto, pass, you'll find yourself at Brixton!
             And *vice versa* — pull it off — you'll be
             As quick as thought — at home, love, to a tea.

Beauty.   Oh, give it me, — I long its power to try.

Beast.   One chaste embrace before you say goodbye!

DUET. — Tancredi.

Beauty.   Embrace you? Oh, dear, no!

Beast.   Ah, say, aren't you content to pare, here, my heart, pray, to
             the core?
             Remember, I do this to please you, all else is naught to me
             now.

Beauty.   Well, to appease you, though 'tis strange, I'll not say no.
                                                        [*He embraces her.*]
Beast.   Oh! say you'll marry me, I
             Can't bear it anymore;
             Say "yes," and all men shall see I

34

Can, for you, the world throw o'er.

Beauty.   I'll tell you some other day,
When I come back – not before;
Don't press me now, dear sir, I pray.
I tremble, oh, dear me! all o'er.
No, no, not now, I tremble, oh, dear me, all o'er!
Let me go now, sir — to Brixton, to Brixton.

Beast.   To Brixton, to Brixton.

Both.   The ring but once fixed on, } you'll find yourself there,
                    } I find myself there.

Beast.   Go, then, away, now, to see thy father.

Both.   Spite o' the distance, you'll (I'll) soon trip it o'er;
The ring will lead her (lead me) to Brixton, speed her (speed me),
And in a jiffy, she'll (I'll) be at the door. [*Exit Beast*, R.]

[*The Scene changes suddenly to the Cottage, as before.*]

Beauty.   This beats the rail-road out and out, I vow.
This *is* a way to ring the changes now!
Here come my sisters! how surprised they'll be!

Enter Dressalinda, Marrygolda, *and* John Quill, *R.*

All.   [screaming.] Oh!

Dressal.   Mercy on us!

Marry.   What is this we see!

Beauty.   Dear sisters, don't you know me!

All.   Oh! a ghost!

Beauty.   No, no! — No spirit from the Stygian coast —
I am your real flesh and blood relation —
So pray subdue this needless consternation!

Dressal.   }
              } Beauty alive!
Marry.   }

John Q.   Fate up again has cast her,
And made all right — Here! Master! Master!
Master! [*Runs out, R.*]

Marry.   I'm all amazement! how did this befal?
Hasn't the Beast, then, eat you, after all?

Dressal.   Has he consented back his prey to render?
Were you too tough? — or has he been too tender!

Beauty.   Where is my father? — let, me calm his fears,
And then I'll tell you all about it, dears.

Marry.   He was half crazy — now he'll be quite wild!

Enter Sir Aldgate *and* John Quill, *R.*

Sir Ald.   Where is my poppet! — where's my precious child?

John Q.   There she is, "all alive, oh," like the eels!

Sir Ald.   Oh, who can tell what a fond father feels, When —

Dressal.   Law, papa, pray don't be so pathetic,
         To me such stuff is worse than an emetic.

Sir Ald.   Well — anything, child, for a quiet life —

Marry.   Come, tell us all – Are you the monster's wife?
         Or is he dead, and left you his sole heiress?

Dressal.   You're dressed as fine as any Lady Mayoress?

Beauty.   I am not married — and he isn't dead.

Sir Ald.   But from the monster have you naught to dread?

Beauty.   If he kills me — 'twill be with kindness merely —
         Would marry me tomorrow — if I chose —
         And gives me — everything you can suppose.

Marry.   He's rich?

Beauty.   As Croesus!

Sir Ald.   Croesus? — Oh — I know,
         He was Lord Mayor of Greece — some time ago —

Dressal.   And wears fine robes?

Beauty.   A Bear-skin—

Dressal.   }
         } How improper!
Marry.   }

John Q.   A BEAR — Bear-skin — a rough wrapper —
         A sort of pilot-coat —

Beauty.   Just so — but here
           I've brought you what you wished for, sisters dear;
           There is your shawl — and there your hundred guineas!

Both.   Oh, thank you! —

Dressal.   [*Aside to Marry.*] Sister — we've been two great ninnies!
           If you or I had volunteered to go,
           We shold have had all this good luck, you know.

Marry.   [*Aside.*] To mar her triumph, let us yet endeavour,
           I hate the odious creature worse than ever.

Sir Ald.   The fellow lives in fine style, I must say —
           Turtle for dinner, no doubt, every day —
           Gad, if I thought he'd hold his horrid jaw,
           I shouldn't mind being Papa-in-law—
           That's if you'd have him, child, — not else, I vow.

Beauty.   But as your ship's come home — you're wealthy now.

Sir Ald.   Oh, no — 'Twas all a hoax about the Polly —
           No matter! — you're alive! — so let's be jolly!
           You are *my* treasure — as my Lady Crackeye
           Said once —

Beauty.   You mean the mother of the Gracchi.

Sir Ald.   Crackeye or Gracchi — it's all one — Let's see
           What *we've* for dinner —

Beauty.   I go back to tea —
           Remember that —

Sir Ald.	Go back!

John Q.	Not come to stay!

Beauty.	Oh, no, I only came to spend the day.
	I must return ere sunset, or the Beast
	Will ne'er forgive me.

Dressal.	[*Aside to Marry.*] There's one chance, at least.
	We'll try and make her overstay the hour,
	And then the Beast will surely her devour!

Sir Ald.	Come all, then — let's be merry while we can.

John Q.	If you're for fun, you know, sir, I'm your man.

GLEE. — (*"Come stain your cheeks."*)
Come o'er, a glass of good brown Sherry,
Let's, while we can, be very merry —

Ladies. Pray, don't get tipsy.
Gents. Only merry. [*Exeunt Sir Aldgate, John Quill, and Beauty, R.*]

Dressal.	Press her to take some negus — then you brew it,
	And pop a little poppy juice into it.

Marry.	I take your hint — I'll dose her, never doubt it.
	[*Exit, R.*]

Dressal.	What fun! — She'll make a precious fuss about it.

AIR. — Dressalinda — (*"Lo! here the gentle lark."*)
Oh! won't it be a lark; here she will rest,
In a dark cabinet, dozing up high,
Until the morning, when, to crown the jest,
She'll be "chawed up most catawampously."

Re-enter Marrygolda, R.

Marry.   I've done the deed! — and hither comes the gipsey!

Dressal.   Where's father?

Marry.   He and John have got quite tipsy.

Dressal.   The sun is setting now — as red as brick —

Marry.   Don't let her see it! — I'll draw the curtains quick!

Re-enter Beauty, R.

Beauty.   Sister — I feel so sleepy, you can't think —

Marry.   [*Aside.*] It works! It works! [*Exit, L.*]

Dressal.   [*Aside.*] "The drink, Hamlet — the drink!"

Beauty.   How goes the time?

Dressal.   Oh, it's quite early yet,
We'll tell you when the sun's about to set;
So, if you'd like to take a nap —

Beauty.   Methinks I'd give the world for only forty winks.

Dressal.   Then why not take them in that easy chair?

Beauty.   If I was sure you'd wake me —

Dressal.   We'll take care —

Beauty.   No — no — I'll drive this drowsiness away —

Dressal.   At any rate, sit down, dear, while you stay.

Beauty.   I'm sure 'tis time — I must be going — going —[*Falls asleep.*]

Dressal.   You're gone, my dear! – and see, the west is glowing
With the last rays of sunset! — Sleep — sleep — sound
I'd not disturb you — for a hundred pound!
[*Exit, L. — The Scene opens at the back, and the Beast appears.*]

AIR. — Beast. — *"All is lost now." —Somnambula.*

All is lost now — Oh, for me, the sun is set forever —
This poor heart in future never
One hope of bliss can see.
Go, ungrateful.
Counted on your word, I had, miss,
Your behaviour's very bad, miss,
It has made me nearly mad, miss,
Quite unhappy, as you may see.
With all confidence appealing,
To any man of feeling,
I'd ask, is this fair dealing?
No! you've used me, madam, really, very ill.
Though my looks might fail to charm you,
Though they rather might alarm you,
Yet I promised not to harm you;
Yes, false one, yes, and I'll keep my promise still.
[*Scene closes. — Beauty seems exceedingly disturbed in her sleep.*]

Enter John Quill *and* Sir Aldgate, R., *both tipsy — John carrying a candle.*

Sir Ald.   John — take care how you go — you'll drop that candle.

John Q.   Never you mind, old Pump — here — where's your handle?

Sir Ald.   John, is this language — to a late Lord Mayor?
         Where is my Beauty?

John Q.   [*Holding the candle to him.*] You may well ask "where —
         Not in your face — it's ugly as a nigger's —
         Not in your form — if I'm a judge of figures!

Sir Ald.   John! — I discharge you —

John Q.   What! — subtract your brains —
         Take me — from you — and pr'ythee, what remains?
         A dry old Pump!
Sir Ald.   Well, well — you'll change this tone!

John Q.   "Well" — Pump, be quiet, and let well alone —
         If you don't know when you've got a good man,
         I know when I've got a good master!
         [*Music, con sordini. — Beauty rises in her sleep and stands up the
         chair.*]

Sir Ald.   [*Starting.*]
         I trust my sight — Back, John — At distance keep,
         Here's Beauty — bolt upright — and in her sleep!

John Q.   Perhaps she's dead — and that's her ghost that's walking! —

Sir Ald.   Horrible thought! — No! hush — I hear her talking.

[*Beauty descends from the chair in imitation of Amina, in the
Somnambula. — The two Sisters enter, L., and are stopped by a sign from
Sir Aldgate.*]

CONCERTED PIECE. — *Sombambula.*

Dressal.	}
Marry.	}
	} Bless us and save us, where is she going now?
Sir Ald.	}
John Q.	}

[*Beauty steps from the chair upon the table.*]
  Over the table. [*She kicks a book off.*] Oh, criky!
    She'll tumble, by jingo!
[*Beauty steps off to another chair, and then to a stool, and then
to the ground.*]

Beauty.   Don't cry, Beast, I'll come back.

Sir Ald.   D'ye hear that, John?

Beauty.   'Tis tea-time, Molly, put the kettle on.

Sir Ald.   Hear her, how she's dreaming, speaking of tea.

Beauty.   Yes, I have lost him, and yet I am not guilty.

All.   Oh, listen.

Beauty.   The ring he gave me, alas! he'll now take from me,
               He'll never let me come out to tea, more.

All.   She wakes!

Beauty.   Where am I? arn't it very late!
               I've overslept myself, as sure as fate!
               It's dark as pitch! Oh, dear, what's to be done?
               There's nothing left me but to cut and run.

Sir Ald.   Dear daughter!

Beauty.   Don't detain me, sir — Goodbye
              To all — Off goes my ring — and off go I!

[*Pulls her ring from her finger — Sir Aldgate, J. Quill,
Dressalinda, and Marrygolda sink through the Stage, as the Scene
changes, and leaves Beauty in the centre of a Grotto in the Gardens of
the Beast's Palace. —Moonlight.*]

Bless me, I don't know where on earth I've got to!
Oh, yonder is the Palace, this the grotto.
But where's its master — Good as he is grim?
Oh, I've forgotten to remember him.
He'll say, where are you, Beast? come out to play,
The moon is shining here as bright as day;
Come with a hoop, if you won't with a call! —
   [*The Leader plays a note or two on his Violin.*]
"That strain again, it had a dying fall,"
And mocked his voice — sweet as a special pleader's.
                    [Leader taps on his desk.]
Was that his tap? — No, it was but the Leader's.
Oh, Mr. —! *— can you my doubts dispel,
And tell me he is safe — and that all's well?

DUET. — Beauty and Leader. — ("*All's well.*")
   Deserted by his Beauty bright,
    Who promised to be back by night,
   The Beast, who saw his hope a wreck,
    Has broken his heart, or else his neck.
   And though a voice salutes her (my) ear,
    'Tis not the one she(I) used to hear.

Beauty.   Where is he? Leader, quickly tell; Above —

---

* Whatever the leader's name may be

Leader.   Below;

Beauty.   All right? —

Both.   All's well.

Beauty.   It's very kind of you, my heart to cheer,
But till I find him, all's not well, I fear!
[*Ascends the Stage, and sees the Beast lying motionless on a piece of rock
in the Grotto.*]

Oh, gemini! — what's here? — Who's this I see,
Stretched in a state of funeral bier? — 'Tis he!
Alas! though I broke mine, he's kept his word.
His must have been the dying fall I heard!
He gave me up — perhaps drank poisoned tea!
And perished — all along of love for me!
Oh, now, indeed, I feel — as 'tis my duty,
That I have been the Beast, and he the Beauty!
Oh, were he but alive again — to pop
The question — I would have him in a —

The Queen of the Roses *appears.*

Queen.   Stop!
Is it a bargain? — Would you really wed
The Beast, if I could prove he wasn't dead?

Beauty.   The lady that I saw once in my sleep?

Queen.   Precisely — Beauty, will you this time keep
Your word, and wed the poor Beast that lies by me,
If I revive him?

Beauty.   Will I? — just you try me

Queen.   Enough! — Behold him in his native land,
           A prince — and yet your servant to command!

[*The Beast disappears as the Scene changes, and discovers Prince Azor upon his Thorne, surrounded by a brilliant Court, Banners, &c. The Prince descends, and kneels to Beauty.*]

Beauty.   What, can this be the Beast?

Queen.   Why this surprise?
           'Tis love hath so improved him in your eyes!
           Where the mind's noble, and the heart sincere,
           Defects of person quickly disappear;
           While Vice — to those who have been taught to hate her,
           Would make, as soon, Hyperion seem a Satyr.

FINALE. — Chorus. — "*Cinderella.*"
           In light tripping measure,
           Surrounded by pleasure,
           We, now, to our own rosy bowers will fly,
           Which care and sorrow dare not come night.

[*Tabelau. — Curtain falls.*]

THE END.